To Nat and Joan,
who have endured so many *quick* little chats,
and to Richard, with love
—A. R.

To Peter, Patrick, Jannick, and my sister, Ulrike,
who I will always carry in my heart
—A. B.

Atheneum Books for Young Readers
An imprint of Simon & Schuster Children's
Publishing Division
1230 Avenue of the Americas
New York, New York 10020
Text copyright © 2005 by Amy Reichert
Illustrations copyright © 2005
by Alexandra Boiger
All rights reserved, including the right of
reproduction in whole or in part in any form.
Book design by Ann Bobco
The text for this book is set in Filosofia.
The illustrations for this book are rendered in
watercolor.
Manufactured in China
First Edition
10 9 8 7 6 5 4 3 2 1
Library of Congress Cataloging-in-
Publication Data
Reichert, Amy.
While Mama had a quick little chat / Amy
Reichert ; illustrated by
Alexandra Boiger.— 1st ed.
p. cm.
"A Richard Jackson book."
Summary: While Rose's mother has a "quick
chat" on the telephone, Rose is supposed to
get ready for bed but finds she is hosting a
party instead.
ISBN 0-689-85170-7
[1. Bedtime—Fiction. 2. Parties—Fiction.
3. Mothers and daughters—Fiction.
4. Stories in rhyme.] I. Boiger, Alexandra, ill.
II. Title.
PZ8.3.R2655 Wh 2005
[E]—dc22   2003019562

WHILE MAMA HAD a QUICK LITTLE CHAT

by Amy Reichert illustrated by Alexandra Boiger

A RICHARD JACKSON BOOK
Atheneum Books for Young Readers
New York   London   Toronto   Sydney

Rrrring! Rrrring! Rrrring!

"Rose, dear," said Mama, "please get ready for bed,
while I have a quick chat with Uncle Fred.
Brush your teeth. Wash your face.
It's getting late!
I want you in bed by
half past eight."

"But, Mama . . . ," Rose sighed, "how long will you be?"

"Not long," Mama promised. "Hurry, let's see
if you are able to do *all* that,
before I finish my quick little chat."

No problem, thought Rose.

But then . . .

Four muscley men said, "Please hold the door.
We've brought your supplies from the party store."
"I'm sorry," said Rose, "but there's no party here."
"Not yet," said the men. "But there soon will be, dear!"

"Mama," called Rose, "could I please talk to you?"

"In a minute," said Mama. "I'm just about through."

So Rose held the door for tables and chairs,
for balloons, twinkle lights, and silverware.

It's hard to believe, but Rose did **all** that,
before Mama had finished her *quick* little chat.

Then . . .

Just as Rose was closing the door,
more people arrived—lots and **lots** more!
They marched right in. They asked, "How do you do?"
They shook Rose's hand. They said, "Nice to meet you!"
"Wait there!" begged Rose. "My mom's on the phone!"
"Don't worry," they said. "We'll be fine on our own."

"**MAAAAAAAAMA!!!**" Rose roared. "I need you **right now**!"

"I'm busy," said Mama. "*You'll* manage somehow."

So Rose did her best to greet each of the guests.
"How do you do?" "Nice to meet you too!"

It's hard to believe, but Rose did **ALL** that,
before Mama had finished her *quick* little chat.

Then . . .

Rose slammed the door shut with a noisy bang.

But as soon as she did, the doorbell rang.

"**MAAAAAAAMA!!!**" Rose yelled.
"Will you *ever* be through?"

"I'm coming!" sang Mama. "In a second or two."

Then waiters rushed in with trays of hors d'oeuvres.
They handed Rose one and said, "Please help us serve."
"There's no party!" cried Rose. "There's no need for food!"
"Feed your guests," they insisted. "You **mustn't** be rude!"
So Rose helped to serve tiny hot dogs
and cream-cheese swirls and big pretzel logs.

It's hard to believe, but Rose did **ALL** that,
before Mama had finished her *quick* little chat.

Then . . .

Something happened that was *really* weird.
From out of thin air—*POOF!*—a magician appeared.
"I'm afraid," he said, "my assistant is sick.
But I'm sure"—he winked—"that you'll do the trick."
"I don't know magic!" said Rose. "I **cannot** help you!"
"It's easy," he told her. "Just follow my cue."

"MAMA!!!" shrieked Rose. "Come **right now** and see!"

"Rose, dear," said Mama, "STOP PESTERING ME!!!"

So Rose was slowly sawed in two,
then magically put back together with glue!

It's hard to believe, but Rose did **ALL** that,
before Mama had finished her *quick* little chat.

Then . . .

Ding! Dong! That dreaded bell! It rang once more.
But Rose was too smart now to open the door,
until she heard someone moan, "Oh, what a bummer!
We brought our drums, but we're missing our drummer!"
Rose threw the door open. "Say, I play the drums!"
Then she beat them and banged them. BUM BUM DITTY DUM!

And everyone there suddenly jumped to their feet
and boogied on down to the sound of her beat!
They shimmied and swayed, they hopped and they bopped
till they couldn't go on, till they just about dropped!

It's hard to believe, but Rose did **ALL** that,
before Mama had finished her *quick* little chat.

But then . . .

Mama yelled, "Rose, dear, I hope you're in bed!
I'm just hanging up now with Uncle Fred!"

"Uh-oh! Oh no!

I'll get in

BIG TROUBLE

if you all don't go!!!"

"So long," said the band. "You drum like a pro.
Your boogie-down beat sure stole the show!"

The magician told Rose she did a great trick.
Then he did another.

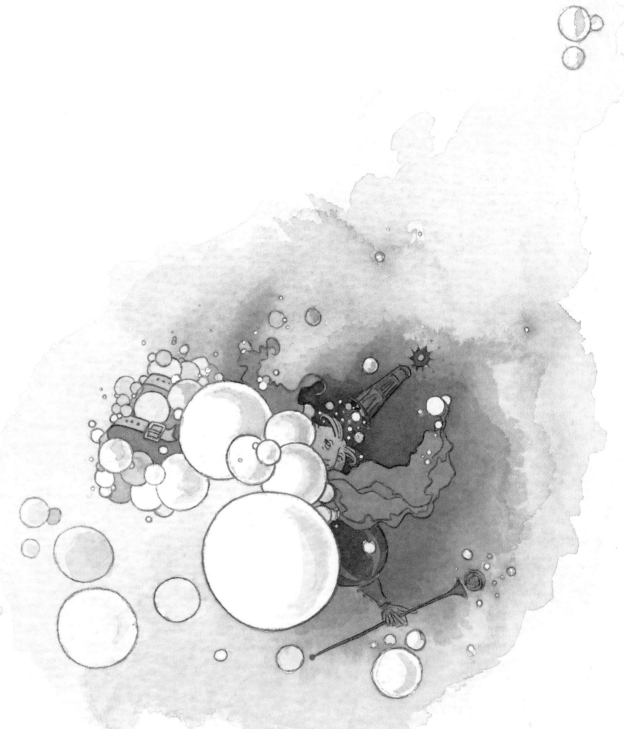

He disappeared—QUICK!

The waiters saw to it that all was put right,
then thanked Rose for helping and bid her, "Good night."

The guests raced out, saying, "Great party! Thank you!!"
"Good-bye!" yelled back Rose, "I had **lots** of fun too!"

Then the four muscley men from the party store
grabbed all their supplies and dashed out the door!

It's hard to believe, but Rose did ALL that,
before Mama had finished her *quick* little chat!

"Rose, dear," called Mama, "I'm finally through!
And I hope that you've done what I asked you to do."

But Rose did not answer; she didn't make a peep.
For Rose was in bed and fast asleep.
"I can't believe it!" said Mama. "Rose did *all* that,
before I finished my quick little chat!"

"Good girl, Rose," whispered Mama.